# Winter Garden

story and pictures by

Ruth Brown

A

Andersen Press

The pale winter moon
shone down on the tree –

– that sheltered the fox –

– who chased the rat –

– which hid from the cat –

– who stalked the birds –

– that landed at dawn
to eat the seeds –

– beneath the tree –

– which grows at the end of our garden.

In the morning they're gone,

but they've been here, I know …

Look – here are the footprints they've left in the snow!